1 MONTH OF
FREE
READING

at

www.ForgottenBooks.com

—————◇—————

By purchasing this book you are eligible for one month membership to ForgottenBooks.com, giving you unlimited access to our entire collection of over 1,000,000 titles via our web site and mobile apps.

To claim your free month visit:

www.forgottenbooks.com/free896560

ISBN 978-0-266-83537-0
PIBN 10896560

THE FARM CREDIT CLUB
Grapevine

Vol. 2	September 8, 1943	No. 27

"OLDEST EMPLOYEE" RELIVES THE PAST

J. L. Gibbs, sometimes known as "old man Gibbs," of Mortgage Corporation Service Division, is one of FCA's "oldest" employees. Gibbs, mellow with years of service, was asked to give the Grapevine reporter a flashback on events and people of the "long ago." As far back as July 1929, Gibbs applied at the Federal Farm Board offices in the Mayflower Hotel. He was hired by Personnel Officer DeVaughn (brother of Sam DeVaughn). Chris L. Christensen, Secretary of the Board, was the first officer to begin work, and he, Myrtle Large (Heavener), and Gibbs composed the first operating staff of the Federal Farm Board.

Gibbs, younger and more spry in those early days, was board room messenger and became well acquainted with members of the Board, whom he respected as "mighty fine men." "Each," Gibbs relates, "was a success in some special branch of farming or industry. Alex Legge, Chairman of the Board, started at the bottom and became president of International Harvester. Sam McKelvie specialized in livestock and made a standing offer of a riding horse to any employee who wanted one and had the facilities to feed it. James C. Stone, the tobacco expert, didn't smoke Lucky Strikes, he smoked Chesterfields. Of course, there were other board members besides these three."

Lunches were prepared in a kitchenette in the Secretary's office. Board members had crates of fruits, vegetables, nuts, etc., sent in from their individual farms. Oranges, lemons, all kinds of fruits were continuously being presented by farmers' organizations. Many of the prize-winning exhibits at county fairs came to the Board.

The "official" car was a 1925 Model-T Ford sedan which belonged to Gibbs (and which he was requested not to park in front of the Mayflower Hotel). The car had cost

(Continued on page 7)

Editorial Staff

Editor	W. S. Harris
Associate Editor	H. T. Mason
Art Editor	T. W. Pritchard
Social Editor	Ann C. Buchanan
Photo Editor	Charles Ritter
Sports Editor	W. S. Hein
Soldiers' News	Inez Barber
Washington Reporter	Dorothy Peffer

Reporters

Mary Jane McGee	Women's Sports
J. S. Kennedy	Discounts
P. L. Rapp	Library
Pat Ross	Dramatics
Vacant	Social Committee
W. R. Slemmons	Legal
Francis W. Smith	Contact Committee
Keith Dellinger	Welfare Committee

Social Reporters

Ralph Miller	Chief Clerk's Office
Anna Messinger	General Files
Amos Russell	Graphic & Duplic.
Dick Robertson	Mail
John Hubble	Purchase & Supply
Gertrude Spear	Stenographic
Catherine Dennelly	Telephone
Dorothy Dick	Vise
R. E. Kaufmann	Planning
Kathryn Price	Cooperative
Ruth Clark	EC & FL Division
Ann C. Buchanan	Examination
Hazel Putnam	F&A
Margaret Ellefson	Cent. Off. Acctg.
Catherine Hardy	Information & Ext.
Lila Stefan	Land Bank
Estelle Oliver	Mortgage Corp.
Mary L. Balsiger	Personnel
Opha Thompson	Production Credit
Leola Teeple	Revolving Fund
Dorothy Heckman	E & CR
Jewell Hill	Intermediate Credit
Claire Katz	Solicitor's Office
Lucille Achauer	Library
Helen Bailey	RACC of Washington
Jeanette Hastings	Governor's Office

FARM CREDIT CLUB WARD

Save the Children Federation has furnished the Farm Credit Club with the description and photograph (which may be seen on the bulletin board) of Ivor Russell, the British child who was adopted at the monthly meeting of the Board of Directors on August 21.

Ivor, one of four children, was born on December 20, 1934. The children live in Kent with their mother, who is an invalid. His father is in the Army and the only income is the Service allowance of L3.25S. The children do a lot to help their mother, even the little girl of 5, and are very cheerful children but are poorly clad and do not have a happy time.

News From Field And Camp

LETTERS FROM OUR MEN AND WOMEN IN SERVICE

John A. Erickson, C. M. (USMS Graduate Station, New York) You probably have begun to wonder why they call us carpenters. Really all we do aboard is to serve as general maintenance men. After 2 weeks training at Sheepshead we were ordered to Baltimore to be aboard the American Navigator, a USMS training ship. It was while aboard this vessel that we gained much practical experience...I surely hope I'm not too long in this place as I'm anxious to be going on my way and be able then to go home for Christmas. It's only about 4 1/2 months away and that could be three or more trips to the Continent.

Lt. N. J. Margaritis. (Camp Mackall, North Carolina) After traveling all over the country for 6 months, your letters and Christmas gift finally came to me. I'm sorry that I neglected to keep you informed about myself but I

2

pe to be able to write more often after is. Unfortunately, there isn't too ch I can say about what has happened me since I joined the Parachute Troops 1941. There hasn't been a Heavy apons Detachment since March last year d I haven't been a private since April st year. When the Army started expand-g its Parachute Troops, I became a aff Sgt., and was with the 504th Para-ute Regiment until September last year which time I went to O.C.S. at the fantry School at Ft. Benning, Georgia. cidentally, it was my old outfit that de the Sicily invasion. That makes 2 my outfits that have seen action frica and Sicily) while I still remain the States...I'm convinced that the ly way to get across is to turn down ery promotion that comes along. I'm ping that I'll be going over with this tfit, when it goes...My commission was ven to me December 19, 1942, and since at time I've been with the 511th. I s instructing troops for several months til I went to the hospital for an opera-on. I stayed in the darn place for months and then I went to Texas on a -day sick leave. When I returned from ave I became a Mess Officer, and I am ch to date. Modestly speaking, I think have a pretty good mess. It's my job write the menus, see that the food properly prepared and in sufficient antities, see that the Mess Hall is pt clean to meet Army sanitary stand-ds. All in all, it is a full-time job. ly one thing wrong with the job - I don't mp as often as the officers in the line ttalions. I've only got 14 jumps in ter nearly 2 years in the Parachute oops. Well folks, I guess this short cry has about covered the wanderings d little experiences of one 2nd Lt. Mar-ritis...Thanks a lot for remembering me th your check and FCA news via the apevine. Regards to all of my old iends at FCA and hello to all the new es I haven't met.

Pvt. George Thomson. (Camp Fannin, Texas) After due consideration of the various factors involved, and with the concurrence of the Army, I decided to come to Texas. This is a brand new camp known as a branch immaterial replacement training center, at which training for new men is given in all branches of the service. I am classified as a "public relations officer," but whether I shall be assigned duties of this nature I do not know as yet. It appears that I must take at least some basic training. This camp is 9 miles north of Tyler in the red-earth country. I haven't seen any thermometers recently, but the tem-perature, I believe, has been 100 or more ever since we arrived. It is bear-able because it is dry heat...The men come from every section of the country - there are even 6 Texans in one of the barracks...Any FCA and personal news will be welcome.

Major H. N. Weigandt. (Pulaski, Vir-ginia) It is over a year ago since I walked out of the FCA building at 13th and The Avenue that very warm day of May 4, 1942, leaving so many staunch friends behind, and yet the time has passed quickly for me and many new things have been unfolded during that time and made a part of my very life. Wish to convey to each and every friend of mine at FCA my most cordial greet-ings. I think of them so many times and wish it were possible to sort of "pop in" for a while to chat. My work keeps me confined in the Third Service Command at present, but there is no telling what the cards hold for us.

Pvt. John K. Smith. (U. S. Army Engi-neers, Camp Abott, Oregon) Gee, guys, this army is a lot of fun. I am in the hardest working best outfit in the whole works. Our job is to get there first, fight off the enemy and at the same time build roads, bridges, airfields, and other necessary accommodations, and leave last...We went on a 5-mile hike today and the guide got lost so it ended up by being about a 9-mile hike. There were about 25 men who passed out completely and nearly all the remainder of them are in bed. As for me, I could start out right now and do it again (?).

PFC Harry E. Martin. (Sioux Falls, South Dakota) The Radio Operator and Mechanics School is located here in Sioux Falls. After I finish I will go to a Gunnery School which lasts for 6 weeks. After that I will be assigned to a bomber and after operational training of about 4 months, we'll go into combat. That's the set-up now; in the Army anything can happen and it usually does...I go to school 6 days a week from 2 a.m. until 10 a.m. Bedtime is 4 p.m. It's a crazy schedule but it does give us more time on our day off. I wish I could drop in and see you. Maybe it won't be so long as we may expect. I think of you all often and remember lots of little things that makes life worth living from around there.

* * *

SERVICEMEN, Don't forget to keep us currently informed of your address. Write the "Grapevine" direct. Some letters to FCA friends never reach the Soldiers News Editor.

* * *

GRASS SEED AVAILABLE AT WHOLESALE PRICES

Wholesale prices at which club members can obtain bluegrass and white clover seed have been posted on the bulletin boards.   (ISD)

FOR UNCLE SAM

Many of our friends from FC
Have abandoned their work a
away -
            Enlisted for Uncle

Unmindful of self, they've
    to fight,
Because they knew well that
    right -
            Freedom for Uncle

Some will be heroes and oth
Many will return, a few die
            Serving our Uncle

Let's breathe them a prayer
    and me,
Whatever they're doing, whe
    be -
            Giving to Uncle Sa

Out of the chaos one day wi
    peace
Victory will triumph and ba
            Victory for Uncle

NEW BOOKS

The Farm Credit Club Libra
recently received the foll
books:

A Tree Grows in Brooklyn b

Without Orders by Martha A

When Hearts Are Li ' ' ' '
    Loring

You Can't Escape by Faith

Tragedy At Law by Cyril Ha

Mary Darlin' by Evelyn Vos

Under Cover by John Roy Ca

4

OMAHA FLB GOES OVER THE TOP ON SUGGESTIONS

Reports of a successful employees' suggestions campaign have been received from Omaha. During a 2-month's campaign the Suggestions Committee received 326 ideas. The Suggestions Committee was composed of the Treasurer and the Secretary of the bank, the supervisor of the Association Service Division, Principal Operations Analyst, and the Assistant to the President. Of the 326 suggestions, 202, or better than 60 percent, were approved. Collectively the suggestions are considered to mark a significant forward step in the way of eliminating nonessentials and discovering better ways to do the job.

At the close of the campaign, each employee who had submitted an approved suggestion received an "I" emblem in recognition of his efforts. The "I" button symbolizes IDEA, INITIATIVE, IMAGINATION, and IMPROVEMENT.

ADVENTURE WITH THE POSTAL GUIDE

Do you get the urge to go wander?
To jump on a freight and just ride?
Then stick yourself to a 3-cent stamp
And get out the Postal Guide.

Do you want Cash and Assurance?
Or Bowlegs and Brandy as well?
It supplies you with Clouds and with Angels,
But just a Half Acre of Hell.

There's a Rat and a Roach in Missouri,
And a Spider in good old Kentuck--
There's a Fox and a Bear, and a Beaver somewhere;
There's even a Moose and a Buck.

There's a Hand and a Foot and an Arm and a Neck
And a Finger in Tennessee,
There's an Eye that is Blue, and a Bone, yes, it's true,
And a Heart and a Thumb, yessiree.

There's a Blue and a Black and a Brown and a Pink,
An Orange, a Green and a Gray--
There are Two and Three Rivers,
Four Lakes and Five Forks
And Twenty-Nine Palms, so they say.

And when you are weary of traveling
And want peace and quiet, by heck,
End up in a place with a short, simple name
Like Antassawamock Neck!   (DEW)

"A GOOD BOOK IS THE PRECIOUS LIFE BLOOD OF A MASTER SPIRIT"

So said the poet Milton. Then why confine your reading to the latest best sellers, when you may choose books that have stood the test of time. Among such books in the club circulating library, you will find the following titles:

Pride and Prejudice by J. Austen
Old Goriot by Balzac
Old Wives' Tale by A. Bennett
Jane Eyre by C. Bronte
Wuthering Heights by E. Bronte
Death Comes for the Archbishop by W. Cather
Lord Jim by J. Conrad
Moll Flanders by D. Defoe
The Red and the Black by Stendhal
Crime and Punishment by Dostoyevsky
Peter Ibbetson by G. DuMaurier
Tom Jones by H. Fielding
Madame Bovary by Flaubert
Forsyte Saga by J. Galsworthy
Return of the Native by T. Hardy
Green Mansions by W. H. Hudson
Sons and Lovers by D. H. Lawrence
Of Human Bondage by S. Maugham
Moby Dick by H. Melville
Gargantua and Pantagruel by Rabelais
Tristram Shandy by L. Sterne
Vanity Fair by H. M. Thackeray
Anna Karenina by L. Tolstoy
Tono-Bungay by H. G. Wells
Ethan Frome by E. Wharton

Central Office Accounting. June Swanson's mother and grandmother from Alcester, South Dakota, recently visited her, and five lucky girls in the apartment enjoyed chicken and chocolate cake prepared by Mrs. Swanson...Week end vacationists include Leona Holland at her home in Sarcoxie, Missouri and Dot Martin with her soldier husband at Sioux Falls, South Dakota...Our best wishes for lots of happiness to Theodora Millemon who was married on August 28 to Cpl. A. L. Stocklos of the Army Air Corps, now stationed at Herrington, Kansas. ...M. J. Fraile has received a card from Lt. Col. H. H. Hendricks with the news that he would soon leave for overseas duties...Maxine Peterson enjoyed a week at her home in Stratford, Iowa, and by strange coincidence Joe McLeish also spent several days in Iowa...The world goes on in spite of a blackout! Friends of Doris and Dick Prewitt are happy to hear that a fine baby boy named Richard, Jr., weighing 6 lbs., 8 oz., was born to them at 10:15 on August 31...Margaret Demaree's vacation was spent in Kansas City...Those still enjoying vacations include W. E. Ludlow in Utah and California, Ladora Robertson at Clinton, Illinois; and Mary Malone in Kansas City.

Chief Clerk's Office. John R. Maguire is the very proud father of a third son named David Michael, weighing 6 lbs., 9 oz., born on August 20.

Cooperative. Vacationist S. D. Sanders has returned from the West Coast... Recent guests of Kay Price were her mother from Kansas and Sally Keeley from Washington, formerly of FCA...Alma Day enjoyed a Sunday at Excelsior Springs...

We note that Cecelia Berry is back in the FCA building with the Dairy & Poultry branch of FDA...N. E. Barker of Memphis was a recent visitor in the central office...A pleasant week's vacation was spent by J. P. Markey at home. ...J. D. Lawrence journeyed to Lincoln, Nebraska, to visit his son in the Air Corps.

EC & FL. Fredda Grantham took the oath of the Marines on September 1...A. W. Walker is on a field trip to Little Rock, Arkansas.

Examination. We hear that Emma Ree Hubbs was sworn into the Army on August 16 and is now a WAC...H. M. Shields' young daughter and her grandparents have returned from a summer in Tennessee... Dorothy Wilson enjoyed a week end with hubby Jimmy at St. Louis, where he is presently stationed...This week's vacationist is Kathryn McCarthy...Dorothy Hagen's soldier fiance suddenly came to town and off they went on a trip to their homes in Illinois...George Bartlett had some interesting experiences on his recent field trip. Ask him to tell you the stories.

FFMC. On September 16, John Nichols will become "Private" Nichols...Byron Hollis will enlist in the Air Corps while in Salt Lake City.

Finance & Accounts. Hervey Veazey spent his week's leave quite profitably. He reports 98 pints of fruits and vegetables canned...The Mehaffys, Sylvia and Del, are swamped with company and hugely enjoying visitors from Idaho, Iowa, and Washington, D. C...Edna Sible is entertaining a friend from Colorado. ...Betty Hooper's wedding date was September 7. She will make her home near Pine Camp, New York, where the groom is presently stationed...Mable Kluttz has been enjoying a visit from her brother, Jerry, of the Washington Post and "Federal Diary" Column...It pays

6

(Continued on page 11)

"OLDEST EMPLOYEE" RELIVES THE PAST
(Continued from page 1)

$50 and did not run consistently. On one trip from the Agricultural Department, with four Board members in it, it chose to stop at the exact center of the intersection at Fourteenth and Pennsylvania Avenue. The four members promptly got out and pushed it over to the curb, where it immediately started again for completion of the journey to the Mayflower.

"After moving to the old Southern Railway building at Thirteenth and E Streets," reminisces Gibbs, "things took on a more businesslike tone in the absence of the former luxurious surroundings. My kitchenette was gone but I had the icebox located in the basement to the left of the east bank of elevators, where we kept the produce that continued to roll in. We once cut a prize-winning watermelon and served the entire staff of the Federal Farm Board."

Gibbs remembers one particularly notable feature of his work with the Farm Board, "There was a spirit of friendliness between officers and employees and, although the Board was reorganized in 1933 under the name of Farm Credit Administration, that spirit wasn't lost because it's still here today."

WRONG NUMBER AT THE RECEPTION DESK

Maxine Lehman, receptionist, had a conversation last week which went like this:

As the phone rang, Miss Lehman picked up the receiver and said, "Information Desk."

No answer.

Miss Lehman (louder): "Information Desk!"

No answer.

Miss Lehman (quite loud): "Information Desk."

Then from the other end came a "Hello," and an elderly woman asked, "Is this the information desk?"

Miss Lehman: "Yes."

Caller: "Well, I want a bushel of grapes. My daughter said you would deliver them to me."

Miss Lehman: "Whom are you calling?"

Caller: "I want a bushel of grapes."

Miss Lehman: "Well, this is Farm Credit."

Caller: "I don't want credit, I want to pay cash for them."

* * *

STORY OF THE WEEK

The man settled down in his office, read his newspaper from cover to cover, and solved the cross-word. Then it was time to knock off. The same thing happened every succeeding day.

During the second week he met his friend, who asked him how he liked the job.

"Fine," he replied. "The office is cozy and warm. I'm quite comfortable, but I don't think they trust me here. Every time I set foot outside the office I'm followed by two young men. They even shadow me when I go to lunch. Am I under suspicion?"

"Not at all," replied his friend. "Those fellows are your secretaries."

* * *

Two WAACs were being followed by a lone G I. Finally one could stand the suspense no longer. Turning to the soldier she ordered, "Either quit following us or go get another soldier."

7

THE DARTS
(With abysmal apologies to "The Raven")

Once upon a noonday weary, as I wandered,
  weak and bleary
Thru the halls of FCA, I chanced to come
  upon a door.
"Club-Room" were the words it listed,
  Though outdoors it rained and misted,
In the clubroom people sported - sported
  as in days of yore.
One game struck my very being.
  'Twas the dart game I was seeing,
Said dart tossed from hand to target,
  neatly placed athwart a door.
Many were the hits and misses.
  Darts were thrown more free than
  kisses,
And my life was near endangered as I
  ducked down to the floor.
Plaster from the walls was chipping
  as the darts went gaily flipping
Past my left ear, off the plaster,
  thence to clash upon the door.
A metal door, so gaily painted,
  heretofore its face untainted
Lost at last its pristine beauty.
  Scratches show now by the score.
Here's the rub, and more's the pity -
  It belongs to Kansas City,
And the council may well protest -
  nay, Perhaps, grow mighty sore.
Gage may hear of the destruction,
  and may raise a potent ruction
Then the dart game, like the Raven,
  will be never, nevermore.

          --Oscar Squink

H. A. CALLAWAY VISITS FCA

Capt. H. A. Callaway, looking chipper
and mighty satisfied with his military
life, dropped in to say hello to central
office folks on Labor Day. He complained
about missing some issues of the Grapevine in his travels but said he would
forgive and forget provided the Club
accepted $1 as a token of appreciation.

PRINCIPLES OF MODERN ART
By Harry Shenker

The murals that are going in the Clubroom are examples of l'art moderne in the
style of the ultra impressionists. This
style is notable for its emphases on balance of volume, balance and opposition
of color, and composition. The objet
principal is to impress the beholder
with living movement, in color and in
form.

In the visual impressions of daily life
we do not see details, we see forms.
Color fills up the form, illuminates the
form, and suggests motion, just as a
drawn line may suggest motion. Realistic
painting does not portray what is usually seen by the eye. It is too micro-
scopic.

Nature is colorful. People are colorful.
All of our surroundings are chromatic
and gay. Then why not express this
color of real life on canvas?

We see in planes and areas of color.
Our baseball player is a representation
of the action, force, and form of a man
outdoors at play. Such a baseball
player, to the trained eye, is a harmony
of color and motion.

BUY AN EXTRA WAR SAVINGS BOND

There are five reasons why you should
buy extra War Savings Bonds during the
Third War Loan Drive to the limit of
your financial capacity:

  1. To help your country.
  2. To back up our fighting men.
  3. To keep prices down.
  4. To build a "nest-egg."
  5. To insure the peace.

Ask your minute man for further details
as to the several series of bonds and
the denominations. BACK THE ATTACK WITH
WAR BONDS. (PIR)

CLUBROOM NEWS

Get that extra midmorning and midafternoon "lift" during your rest periods by eating a nutritious candy bar from the vending machine in the clubroom. Those good Planters Peanuts are there also.

* * *

Don't forget, there's a cigarette vending machine in the clubroom for your convenience.

* * *

Carrie D. Meador has been supplying the clubroom with back issues of the "Reader's Digest" and "Life" magazines. Many thanks!

STAY AT HOME WITH A GOOD BOOK

The Farm Credit Club circulating library has moved to the new clubroom on the first floor on the southwest side of the building. Members may borrow the outstanding new books, both fiction and nonfiction, at the rate of 5 cents for 3 days and 2 cents for each day thereafter. If you have any suggestions for the purchase of new books not already on the shelves, drop them in the suggestion box in the clubroom.

THOUGHTS ON LABOR DAY

Holidays we kept in view
To do just what we wanted to--
But now we can't do what we would,
We spend them for the Nation's good.

New Year's Day you had to rue
The stuff that wasn't good for you--
The birth of Washington was fun
Because you lay in bed 'til one--
You packed a lunch Memorial Day
And ate it shooing bugs away--
The glorious Fourth, with sun & noise,
You burned your nose & lost your poise--
Labor Day you had to spend
To watch that summer romance end--
Thanksgiving Day you ate like sin
(Before point rationing came in!)
Though Christmas Day you do receive,
In Santa Claus you can't believe.   9

We liked our holidays, that's true,
But think of all the good we do--
So holidays we do not miss--
(I know that I'll get slugged for this!)
(DEW)

GARDEN FESTIVAL TO BE HELD SEPTEMBER 29

As an appropriate finale to the garden shows which have been held during the summer, the Victory Garden Committee is planning to hold a Garden Festival on Wednesday, September 29. The demonstration will include exhibits of fresh, canned, and dried fruits and vegetables, and cut flowers. Prizes will be awarded for the most outstanding exhibits in each of the four categories.

Final arrangements and rules of the Festival will be printed in the next issue of the Grapevine, but the following plans are already definite:

1. Fresh fruits and vegetables and cut flowers grown in the exhibitor's garden will be auctioned.

2. Canned and dehydrated fruits and vegetables will not be auctioned unless the exhibitor so desires.

3. All items for exhibit should be placed in the Conference Room (2203) early during the morning of September 29.

4. The show will be open from 11:30 to 12:15 at which time the auction will take place.

Because of the large volume of exhibits which is likely to be submitted, the Victory Garden Committee urges each prospective exhibitor to fill out the accompanying blank and return it to Irvin Dyke, room 4025. At the same time, note the date of the Festival on your calendar. If you have any questions or suggestions regarding the final plans for the Festival call Mr. Dyke or Richard Kaufmann.   (ISD)

SCRAP FOR VICTORY

Top honors for collecting scrap in the industrial and business area of Kansas City go to Area 6. This area, consisting of 13 city blocks, was divided into two sections, with Captain Richard Kaufmann in charge of section 1, and Captain L. G. Simonds in charge of section 2. The lieutenants were all Farm Credit men.

If medals were being awarded, every one of the 16 lieutenants who actually gathered scrap would deserve one. And if commissions were the reward, several of our top-flight lieutenants would now be captains. Through their efforts 146,759 pounds of scrap were gathered in. This figure represented substantially larger quantities than those produced by areas of similar size and type, as well as the highest quantity of donated scrap produced by any team in the city. In addition, the area ranked seventh in greater Kansas City, in competition with industrial areas which produced commercial scrap in carload lots.

This is just another instance which proves that Farm Credit employees are right in there doing their part. Our thanks to Wayne Morris, Kenneth Richmond, Francis Smith, Gordon Smith, Larry Waugh, Carl Bark, Leslie Surginer, Walter Hein, M. R. Hoberecht, Raymond McWhirt, George A. Meyer, M. J. Fraile, Irvin Dyke, G. P. Walker, Torrence Cease, and Fulton Want.   (JDC)

NEWS FROM MAE LATCHFORD

Mae Latchford, a former employee of the Cooperative Division who is now employed by the Rubber Development Corporation, recently wrote of a few of her experiences while in Brazil:

"I left Manaos last Friday morning at an early hour and had a most delightful plane ride to Belem. We stopped at Santaren for lunch. It is a typical native town and I would have liked to have had a chance to do some shopping, but only stayed there for an hour. The day was an ideal day for flying and we reached Belem around 3. I like Belem so much better than Manaos, although it does rain here nearly every day. The weather was ideal in Manaos and we had very little rain. A room had been reserved for me at the Grande Hotel...I can now appreciate how far up the jungles I was in Manaos and how very primitive the living is there....

"The Grande Hotel is modern in every way—in fact, Belem reminds one of a tourist city. I have not had a chance to do much sightseeing...We have music at lunch and dinner and they always play American music and dedicate it to some lady in the dining room...In our office we have almost all Brazilians but I am in the room with two American men who speak our language all the time. Our window looks out over the city and it is a very pretty sight with the palm and date trees in the distance...

"Sunday the office had a picnic and I was invited. It was typically native but I am now used to eating Brazilian food. We roamed through the woods and after walking until our feet hurt, sat on a log, when we heard a peculiar noise, looked up and saw some monkeys...

"I must tell you about my farewell party at my Brazilian teacher's. Her home is one of the prettiest I have ever been in. She has a beautiful baby grand piano and plays beautifully. She speaks English fairly well. There were about 10 people there and I must say I have never been entertained in an American home with more poise and grace."   (KD)

to advertise. After viewing a moving picture on how to play golf, Warren Thompson immediately went out and purchased a new set of clubs...Alene Foster's handsome son from Pawnee City, Nebraska, has been visiting her. Present vacationists include Margaret Meunier with relatives at St. Paul and in North Dakota; Carrie Rountree at her home in Kansas City; Maude Freeman at her home in Washington; Meda Martin at Springfield, Missouri, and other places; Lorraine Morava with friends and family at Lincoln and Wilbur, Nebraska; and the Meuers girls, Bernice, Lorraine, and Yvonne at Rockaway Beach.

General Files. Julia Connor is vacationing at Trenton, Missouri. On a Saturday eve before she left, Kathleen Thomas and Alvina Preinkert entertained with a lovely little bridge party for her... Kenneth Whitaker and Kenneth Epperson are "off to the war." - Mr. Whitaker in the Navy and Mr. Epperson in the Army... Roberta Harlan is leaving to accept a position at Portland, Oregon.

Governor's Office. Martha Head entertained with a delightful breakfast in honor of Jeanette Walker whose entrance in the Marines on September 6 was preceded with a lively auction of her wardrobe and a presentation of many useful gifts...We welcome Lillian Burch who came from F&A to the office of Robert McConnaughey...A visiting lieutenant and a birthday luncheon at the Kansas City Club may account for Mary Lou Vance's excited mood...Many cigars and boxes of candy announced the arrival of Irvin Dyke's son, "Terry."...Congratulations to Arthur Rogers who recently returned from a "successful" vacation, a married man...Dorothy Dyhrberg has returned from a pleasant week in Omaha...Ann Cowan has received word that her brother who has been convalescing in North Africa has returned to his company...Jeanette Hastings is enjoying a week in Alexandria, Louisiana.

Graphic & Duplicating. Composing Unit is having a fast turnover. At the same time Olive Russell left us for the Payroll Office, Rita Nordhus became a new member of our group. We have lost Harold Yeager to Pratt & Whitney Aircraft and Harman Hercules to the Aluminum Company of America...Georgie Arnold is vacationing in Kansas City.

Information & Extension. Joan Muilman entertained several of the girls with a delightful outdoor picnic on the lawn of her home.

Intermediate Credit. Mrs. Evelyn Black's daughter, Lynn, has returned from a pleasant summer with her grandmother in Alexandria, Virginia...M. H. Uelsmann's daughter, Elizabeth, is home from a summer spent in Mexico where she studied Spanish. Miss Uelsmann is a student of the Randolph-Macon Women's College at Lynchburg, Virginia.

Land Bank. Our latest word from Cpl. Gertrude Grove is from Santa Ana, California, where she has transferred as radio instructor and stenographer. She marvels at sleeping under 2 blankets after the heat of Las Vegas...After a month's vacation in Washington, D. C., and Alabama, Sally Tacker bid adieu to her husband who was called into the service...We hear that Lila Owens is having a grand vacation down in Missouri. ...Week end vacationists include Marjorie Hinds in Topeka, Kansas, and Louise Plack at home in Kansas City with that adorable youngster of hers...Ask Orella Yeager to tell you her bee story!

Library. A welcome is extended to our new employee, Juanita Akers...We hear that Kenneth Rice is happy in a permanent assignment to the Quartermaster Corps at San Francisco.

Mail. Harvey Miller has returned from a pleasant vacation. During Harvey's

(Continued on page 12)

11

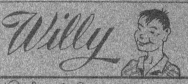

Willy

Well, Ma, this plais just gets fassynatiner and fassynatiner. You remember
about the sochable club I wrote you.
I guess the officers are running for
election again, because they sure been
spending the doozepaiers money.

Now we have a sochable room, and is it
sochable. They is rugs on the floor and
pitchers on the wall and lownges all over
the plais made out of this shiny water
pipe and oilcloth stuff. They is books
along one wall in closed bookceises so
they wont get dusty, and they is a
cupple of little rooms whear they have
tables where you can eat or play pea-
nuckle.

The whoal thing is done in the best bar-
room modern, and it just naiks you
thirsty to go in there, and then there
ain't nothing to do but sit down and
read a magazine and keap an eye out for
yore boss.

However, they got a very nice arrainge-
ment here. You are only supposed to
talk 45 minutes for lunch, and the
theery is, of coarse, that you will bolt
yore lunch like a dog so you can sit
around the club room for half an hour
wishing you hadn't eat so fast. But
nobuddy knows when to go to lunch
except when he's hungry. I been feel-
ing silly about going at 10 o'clock
but I got a lot of company and nobuddy
notices if I go at 12 again, but what I
started to say was they keap the club
room open about three hours and no

matter what time you g
you can always say, I
from lunch. All you n
a farely fresh toothpi

Yo

STRICTLY PER
(Continued from

absence, Charles Tomps
chauffeur...Wilma DeBo
Personnel Files...We w
bers to our section, M
and James Mauer...We a
have with us Jane Nevi
from the Stenographic
Johnson has left to at
versity.

Personnel. Matilda Hu
from Ohio wearing a spa
ring, the gift of Sgt.
Paul is spending an ext
in the States after 2 ½
Friends were glad to s
Wienberg when he recent
a visit enroute to spen
his "home in Wyomin'."
cent is on a field tri
Virginia Baker has retu
weeks' vacation on her
Pleasant, Iowa...John
announce the arrival o
7 lbs., 14 oz. girl, w
September 4...A baby b
7 lbs., 15 oz., was bo
Carl Cockrum on Septem

Personnel Files. Nadi
ing a visit with her p
Missouri.

Production Credit. We
Mae Reed and Chloe Ful
fold after several mon
J. F. McAdam is recove
an operation.

12

...ioning in Missouri satisfaction. He ost got his fill of "fried chicken."... detailed to the ut is presently vaca- hall and James Brack- ... We hear that James nsin...We are glad to :ephens, a new member Kenneth Lowe, formerly ...Virginia Paine has the Mail Section.

It was a very at took Margaret Ster- ls, Texas. She will a certain staff ser- :o Ida Bernstein who vith the Commodity on September 1... a resigned on August 31 in Los Angeles.

arolyn Portmann sit with hubby Bill rlough from Ellington

. We welcome George attorney's staff. formerly with FCA)ffice in Wichita... retches will be that she has trans- r Department at Inde- , to the Solicitor's ›n...Warren Slemmons ationing at Oconomowoc Jacationists who are s include Margaret Por- , and Etha Townsend... iia Jones Krohta and ll honeymooning at , where he is pres- 3arbara Frank and :rie, Pennsylvania.

Office in Denver. Mr. Gilbert will be joined in about a month by Lela.

Stenographic. Best luck to Betty Jean Funk who has resigned to further her education at the University of Kansas City...Jessie Maddux was unexpectedly called to Enid, Oklahoma, because of the illness of her sister...Faye Hanley week-ended at her home in Paris, Missouri ...A Missouri vacationist is Ellen Jane Beery who is spending her time at Inde- pendence...Marjorie Freel enjoyed a sur- prise visit with her brother, Capt. W. I. Freel, of Purdue University, Lafayette, Indiana...Other travelers include Muriel Koll who is enjoying a visit with her folks in New Orleans and Maurine Kava- naugh who will spend some time in Los Angeles.

Telephone. It was nice to see Marine Mary McBride when she recently stopped over enroute to her home in Kansas...A late announcement! On August 8, Lois Ehman became the bride of Wayne Hill of the Navy. A very lovely lamp was the gift of the girls in the section.

OUR WASHINGTON REPORTER

S. U. Baxter dropped in to say that the 14-page August 25 issue of the Grapevine hints somewhat that it might later develop into a book form!...The August 31 issue of the USDA Employees' News Bul- letin carried a correction to the effect that FCA, not SCS, was the first unit in the Department to go over the top in the purchase of war bonds with a goal of "90 and 10."...Captain Nephtune Fogelberg dropped in to say he was glad to be back in Washington...Cpl. J. D. MacWilliams is now stationed in England with the Army Air Corps...Shirley Lupton is in Nebraska, where her husband is in the service...

Among vacationists in CR&S Division are Mr. Bain (spending his time painting - so we are told); Bea Dragon (ask her how much farming she did down there in Virginia); and Edward Ballow (he wouldn't say where he spent his). September also brings three losses to CR&S. Mildred Sundquist has resigned to return to teaching in Michigan; Carol Collins is planning to attend George Washington U; and Mary Buckley transferred to BAI... James C. Moore has at last decided to make Washington, D. C. his home - he recently brought his family here from Corvallis, Oregon...Incidentally, L. N. Conyers gave us a glowing account of the new clubroom out there - too bad we can't dash out and see same!

THERE'S A NEW MAN IN THE CLUBROOM, GIRLS!

I wish I had muscles like Oscar,
And a beautiful rosy complexion--
As he stands there all day
In his own quiet way,
In a mood of such silent reflection.

And oh, for the waistline of Oscar!
For that hour-glass figure I languish--
It can surely be said
That Federal Spread
To Oscar will never cause anguish.

I wish I had color like Oscar,
With shade 'neath my hat-brim so mellow--
But I'm sure, if I knew
That my features were blue,
I also would blush red and yellow!
(DEW)

TANDEM

Ruth rode on my tandem bike

Directly back of me -

I hit a bump, but did not stop,

And rode on ruth-less-ly.

Harry Shenker's Clubroom murals are genoowine art. Have to be careful what you say about them to avoid criticizing yourself--like that visitor to the Louvre who looked at all the pictures and told the museum attendant he didn't like them. "Monsoor," replied the attendant, "you have made a mistake. It is you who is on trial, not the pictures."

14

To: Irvin Dyke, Room 4025

I desire to enter items in the following classifications in the
Garden Festival scheduled for Wednesday, September 29 (Please
check each group in which you plan to exhibit):   .

☐ Fresh fruits and vegetables   ☐ Dehydrated (dried) fruits
                                        and vegetables

☐ Canned fruits and vegetables   ☐ Cut flowers

      Name . . . . _ _ _. Room

Sportlight

GOVERNOR BLACK SETS THE PACE FOR THE OPENING OF THE MEN'S BOWLING LEAGUE

The FCA men's bowling league started its 11th season Monday evening, September 6, 1943, on the terrace lanes at the Plaza Bowl. A large gallery of FCA employees witnessed a perfect strike bowled by the Governor, thereby starting eight teams on their way to a 32-week schedule. Graphic opened up with Mortgage Corporation and made a clean sweep of all 3 games by a wide margin. Porter's 471 was tops for both teams. Harris Willingham and John Plott with 410 and 414, respectively, represented high sets for the Mortgage Corporation. Administrative captured the odd game from a rejuvenated Legal team. Schlick and McClurg, with 449 apiece, took high honors in this match. President Tom Piper was a little shaky after the formalities and bowled a snappy 78 for his first game offering. Accounts, with Ward as a new member of their team, squared off on the Reports Five for 2 close wins. This contest saw Hein go from one extreme to the other by opening up with a 110 game and coming back in the second stanza with 218. His set of 480 topped both teams. Land Bank's veteran bowler, Max Menk, polished the maples for 523. This, coupled with Morrison's 489, enabled the Land Bankers to take 2 from the Coops. Frazee's first offering was a blistering 79; however, he improved in his next 2 games. Commissioner Sanders was high for the Coop team.

TEAM STANDINGS

Team	Won	Lost	Total Pinfall
Graphic	3	0	2,015
Administrative	2	1	2,132
Land Bank	2	1	2,120
Accounts	2	1	2,045
Reports	1	2	2,161
Legal	1	2	1,909
Cooperative	1	2	1,762
Mortgage Corporation	0	3	1,769

RECORDS

H T G	Administrative	801
H T S	Reports	2,161
H I G	Hein	218
H I S	Menk	523

AVERAGES

Menk	174-1	Hein	160
Morrison	163	Porter	157

WOMEN BOWLERS START SEASON

The FCA women's bowling league returned to the Pla-Mor Alleys for their 1943-44 season, starting Wednesday evening, September 8, 1943, on a 27-week schedule. Ten teams make up the league: Land Bank, Purchase, Audit, Reports, General Files, Legal, Stenographic, Finance and Accounts, Personnel, and Securities.

PAT CLARK SHOOTS A GROSS 86 IN THE OPENING ROUND OF THE WOMEN'S GOLF TEAM PLAY

The FCA women's golf team play started its first round on September 5. Pat Clark, with a nice gross 86, coupled with Alzada Harbert's 101, took 4 points from the Luella Cogswell - Gertude Roeh duo. Alma Franklin and Meda Martin were able to run away with 6 points from the high-scoring team of Edna Sible and Corene Nelson in spite of Edna's 30-foot sinker.

putt on the 18th hole. In the match between Gertrude Foerster - Eileen Hague vs. Lucille Holmes - Vivian Anderson, the former team, with the aid of Gertrude's new acquisition from Lowe and Campbell and Hague's low score of 99, breezed through for all 6 points. The match between Alice Morgan - Pat Ross and Delta Vaughn - Sylvia Mehaffy teams will be played this week.

THE MEN'S GOLF TEAM PLAY ENTERS ITS LAST TWO WEEKS

The team of Fowler and Plott holds a commanding lead in Division A while Lindsey and Menk, with two matches to play, lead Division B.

TEAM STANDINGS
SEPTEMBER 8, 1943

Team	Matches played	Points won	lost	%
DIVISION A				
Fowler - Plott	5	22	8	733
Gray - Burkett	4	16	8	667
Warburton - Spelman	4	14	10	583
Mason - Dellinger	4	13	11	542
Moore - Smith	5	13	17	433
Bark - Hein	3	6	12	333
Watt - Mills	3	0	18	000
DIVISION B				
Lindsey - Menk	4	21	3	875
Light - Howard	4	18	6	750
Ward - Holmes	5	22	8	733
Thompson - Hume	5	13	17	433
Lockwood - Collins	4	9	15	375
Armacost - Guill	4	5	19	208
Kraus - Jacomet	4	2	22	083

VITAMIN PURCHASE PLAN

A committee of the Farm Credit Club has been investigating group purchase of vitamins. Very attractive competitive prices have been obtained on a multiple vitamin capsule, conditioned on the purchase of 100,000 capsules, and a capsule containing vitamin A & D concentrate, conditioned on a purchase of 50,000 capsules.

The multi-vitamin capsule will sell for less than $2 per hundred. Final prices are now being arranged. This vitamin ordinarily sells for $6 or more per hundred capsules. Some sample 50-capsule bottles furnished to the committee which were taken from the shelves of a retail store bore a price mark of $3.89.

Each capsule will contain the following percentages of the minimum daily vitamin requirement for adults which has been established by the Food and Drug Administration. (The minimum daily requirement is the amount just sufficient to prevent conditions signifying outright deficiency.)

Vitamin A - 120%

Vitamin B_1 - 300%

Vitamin B_2 - 100%

Vitamin C - 100%

Vitamin D - 120%

These quantities of the vitamins named, when taken in combination with a normal diet, will ordinarily raise the total vitamin intake to the optimal intake. (An optimal intake is the best or most favorable quantity of vitamins.)

Additional information and an opportunity to order your family's winter supply of vitamins at an exceedingly favorable price will be offered in the near future.